Mickey and the Pet Shop Pup

"Have a good time," called Mickey. Mr. Palmer
was leaving for an overnight trip and he asked
Mickey to take care of his pet shop while he was gone.
"This will be a snap!" Mickey said.
"A snap!" repeated Mr. Palmer's pet parrot.

Mickey gazed at the cuddly pets and colorful fish. They all seemed content—all but one, that is. A cute little puppy was whining and whimpering in the saddest way.

"Poor little fella," said Mickey. "What you need is some attention."

Mickey lifted the puppy from the kennel.

"Steady, boy," said Mickey. But the lively puppy wriggled free and raced over to the goldfish bowl for a drink.

"Watch out!" screeched the parrot.

But he was too late. The bowl tumbled to the floor with a crash.

"Uh-oh!" cried Mickey.

"Crash! Crash!" squawked the bird, furiously flapping his wings.

"Gotcha!" Mickey caught the fish and put it in a new bowl.

Mickey put the puppy back in the kennel. "Now you can't cause any more trouble."

Just then he heard the door open and in walked his first customer.

"Can I help you?" Mickey asked.

But before the customer could answer, the puppy got free again and opened the door to a cage of mice.

"Eeek! I'll come back later. Much later!" cried the customer as she raced for the door.

Mickey gathered up all the pets and put them back where they belonged.

"Don't worry, little guy," he said. "Someone will buy you. You'll see."

That night the puppy howled at the top of his lungs. Mickey covered his ears with a pillow, but it didn't help.

It wasn't long before the puppy got exactly what he wanted—a cozy spot under the covers, right next to Mickey!

When Mickey woke up the next morning, the store was a mess! Worse still, he couldn't find the puppy anywhere!

Mickey searched high and low for his little friend. Finally he caught sight of a wriggling bundle of fish food.

Mickey looked inside the bag.
"There you are!" he exclaimed happily. "I guess all you wanted was some breakfast."

"Well," sighed Mickey, "I guess I should clean up the store."

As he worked, the puppy trotted along beside Mickey, helping out wherever he could.

"You may be a rascal," said Mickey, "but I am getting used to having you around."

Mickey had just finished when in strode Mr. Palmer.
"It looks like everything went smoothly," he said,
handing Mickey his paycheck.
"Easy as pie," replied a very tired Mickey.

Mickey was about to leave when the puppy began to howl and scratch at the door of his kennel.

"I'm going to miss you, too, little fella," said Mickey sadly.

Suddenly Mickey thought of the perfect solution. He'd take the pup instead of the pay! Everybody was very happy—especially the parrot, who screeched, "And don't come back!"

"But what should I call you?" Mickey wondered.
Just then, he saw a newspaper headline:
NEW PICTURES OF PLANET PLUTO!
"That's it! I'll call you Pluto!" exclaimed Mickey.
Pluto gave his new master a big wet kiss, and from
that day on, Mickey and Pluto were the best of friends.